All About Mars

Cameron Macintosh

Contents

All About Mars

The Red Planet

Mars is the fourth planet from the Sun in our **solar system**, which is part of the Milky Way **galaxy**. From Earth, Mars often looks like a red star. Because of this, it has become known as "the red planet".

For thousands of years, people around the world have been fascinated by Mars. It has featured in the stories and myths of many cultures, including some First Nations cultures in Australia, New Zealand and North America.

The red planet is named after the ancient Roman god of war, called "Mars". This is an artist's impression of Mars, the Roman god.

From Earth, Mars can be seen with the naked eye.

Mars is the fourth-closest planet to our Sun. The closest planets to the Sun are Mercury, Venus and Earth, in that order. Earth is about 149 million kilometres from the Sun, while Mars is about 228 million kilometres from the Sun.

Mars is the fourth planet from the Sun.

Like Earth and the other planets, Mars is always **orbiting** the Sun. It moves around the Sun in an **elliptical** path. This means that it does not orbit in a perfect circle, but rather in a slightly stretched circle, like the shape of an egg. It comes closer to the Sun at different points in its orbit.

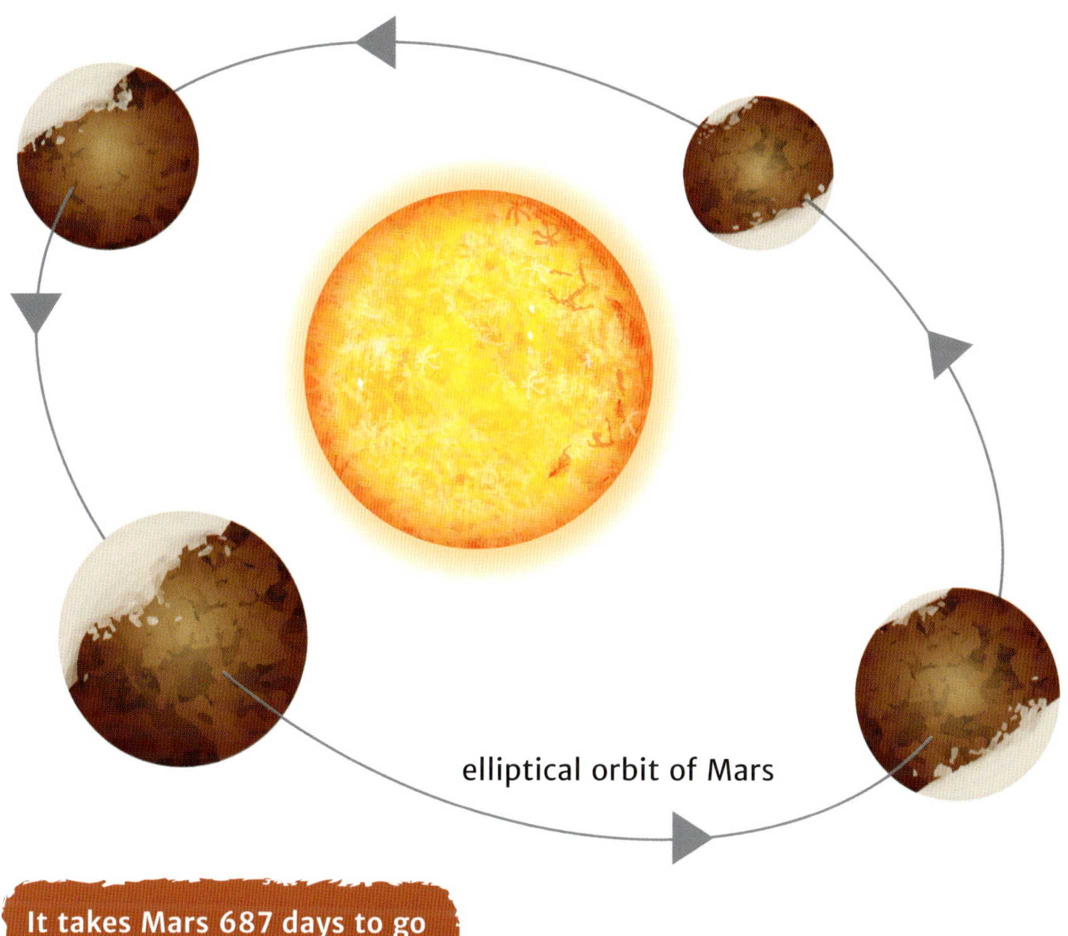

It takes Mars 687 days to go all the way around the Sun.

Mars is about 6790 kilometres in **diameter** from one side to the other. It is about half as wide as Earth.

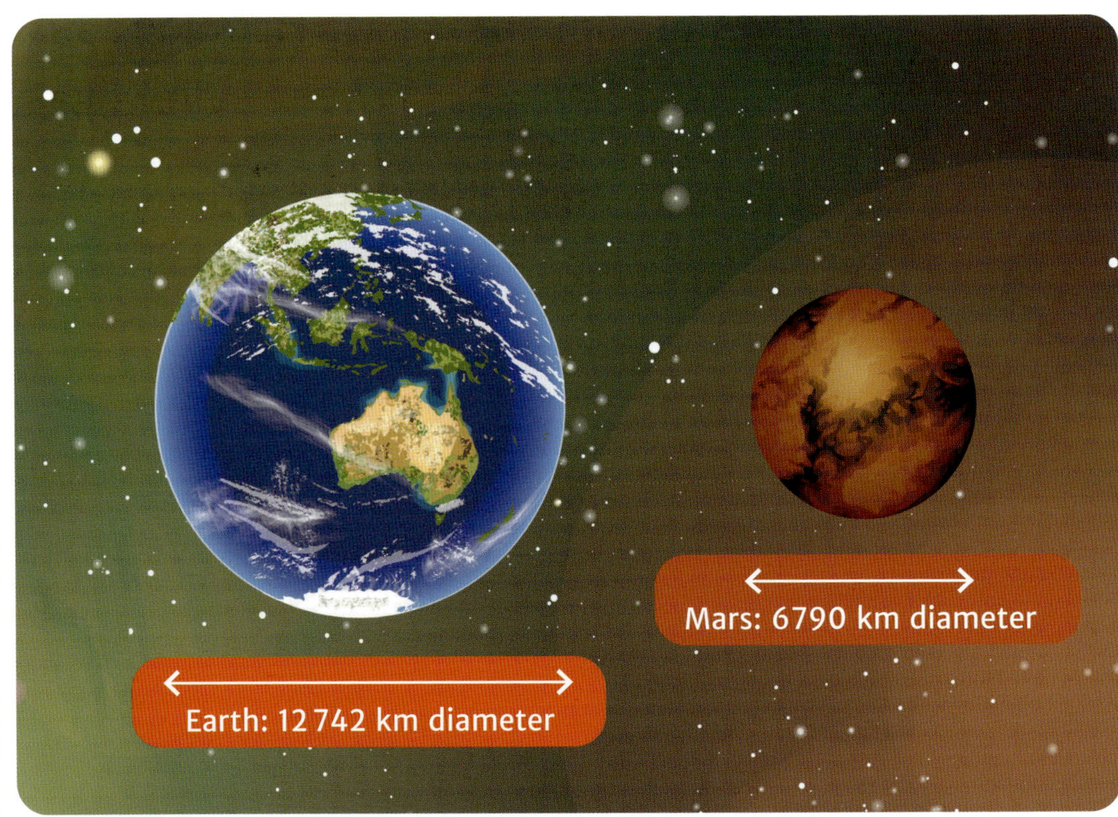

Mars is the second smallest planet in the solar system. It is only half the size of Earth.

Mercury is the only planet in the solar system that is smaller than Mars. Most of the other planets are much bigger, especially Jupiter, Saturn, Uranus and Neptune. However, compared to the Sun, all of the planets in the solar system are tiny.

Mars is a rocky, dusty planet, but it is like Earth in many ways. It spins around, like Earth does, and has many mountains and valleys. Mars also has many **extinct** volcanoes. At both of its poles, north and south, it has ice caps. These are large areas of frozen, salty water.

Billions of years ago, the surface of Mars was largely covered by oceans. Scientists have observed riverbeds and canyons made there long ago by moving water.

an extinct volcano on the surface of Mars, seen from above

Mars and Its Moons

Mars has two small moons: Phobos and Deimos. Phobos is the larger of the two moons. It is much smaller than Earth's moon. It looks more like a pile of rubble with craters than a **spherical** moon like ours. Deimos has an irregular shape, too, but has fewer craters than Phobos.

Nobody knew Phobos or Deimos existed until 1887. In that year, **astronomers** spotted them from an **observatory** in Washington DC, in the USA.

Scientists used the Great Equatorial **telescope** at the United States Naval Observatory in Washington DC, USA, to discover Mars's two moons.

A Rusty, Dusty Planet

Mars looks red from Earth because of the red rocks and dust that cover most of its surface.

This red colour comes from the iron oxide in the rocks and dust. Iron oxide is another name for rust. It forms when iron and oxygen mix together with water. This occurred millions of years ago on Mars, when there was more oxygen on the planet. Now, there is only a tiny amount of oxygen in Mars's **atmosphere**.

Photos taken on Mars show its red, rocky surface.

Many of the rocks on the surface of Mars are made of basalt. Basalt is a type of rock that comes from volcanoes.

Basalt rock on Earth is made from the dried lava from volcanoes.

The surface of Mars can shake violently, like an earthquake. These shakes are known as "Marsquakes". Scientists think they may be caused by large cracks on the surface of Mars. Sometimes, tension builds up between these cracks, causing violent shakes.

This is an aerial view of a large crack in the surface of Mars.

The Climate on Mars

Because of its red colour, many people think Mars is a hot planet. The opposite is true – it is very cold most of the time.

Parts of Mars can warm up to about 20 degrees **Celsius**, but this does not happen often. Most of Mars stays well below freezing throughout the year. In some places, it can be as cold as -153 degrees Celsius.

The surface of Mars can get extremely cold, with ice in some places.

Mars is colder than Earth because it does not have an atmosphere that can trap the Sun's heat like Earth does. It is also colder because it is further from the Sun, and the Sun's rays become cooler the further they travel.

Like Earth, Mars has seasons, which make different parts of Mars warmer and cooler at different times of the **Martian** year. The ice caps at its poles grow or shrink depending on the season. Mars also has clouds, but they are very thin and don't shed rain.

Mars has polar ice caps at its north and south poles, like Earth.

Studying Mars

People have studied Mars for thousands of years. The earliest recorded observations of Mars took place in Egypt, about 4000 years ago.

Around 3000 years ago, Chinese astronomers made records detailing the movements of Mars. At around this time, **Babylonian** astronomers were studying Mars, too. They used mathematics to track and **predict** the movements of Mars and other planets in the night sky.

Ancient Chinese astronomers studied the planets and stars.

This hand-powered computer (left) made from bronze gears was likely used by the ancient Greeks to predict the position of the planets in the sky. Scientists have rebuilt it today (right).

Over the centuries, Mars was also studied by Greek and Indian astronomers and mathematicians. About 2500 years ago, Greek scientists worked out that Mars was further away from Earth than the Moon. Around 1600 years ago, Indian astronomers made a close estimate of the size of Mars.

The ancient Greek philosopher Aristotle saw that Mars could be hidden when the Moon passed in front of it, which meant it was further away than the Moon.

Mars Through Telescopes

A big leap forward in the study of Mars happened in 1610. In that year, Galileo Galilei, an astronomer and mathematician in Italy, became the first person to observe Mars through a telescope. He noticed that Mars was not perfectly round.

Galileo Galilei

In this painting from 1858, Galileo Galilei shows the leader of Venice how to use a telescope.

In 1636, Francesco Fontana, another astronomer from Italy, made the earliest-known drawings of Mars, using observations he had made through a telescope.

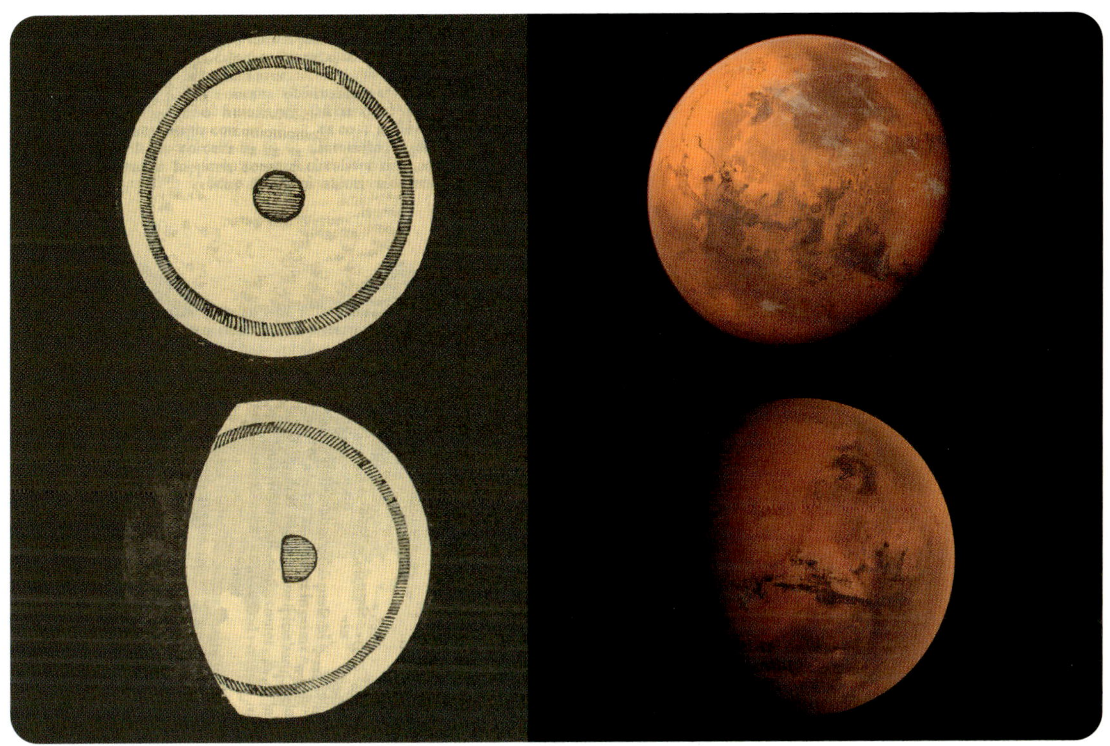

Francesco Fontana's early drawings can be compared to modern photos of Mars.

In 1672, another Italian astronomer, Gian Domenico Cassini, became the first person to calculate the distance between Earth and Mars.

In 1782, the British astronomer William Herschel observed the white areas around the poles of Mars. He was the first person to realise that they were made of ice.

Exploring Mars with Spacecraft

A new era in the exploration of Mars began in the 1960s, when the first spacecraft were sent there. *Mariner 4*, launched by **NASA**, took the first close-up photos of Mars's surface.

In the 1970s, the first two spacecraft landed on the surface of Mars. These spacecraft, known as *Viking 1* and *Viking 2*, had cameras to study the soil and look for signs of life.

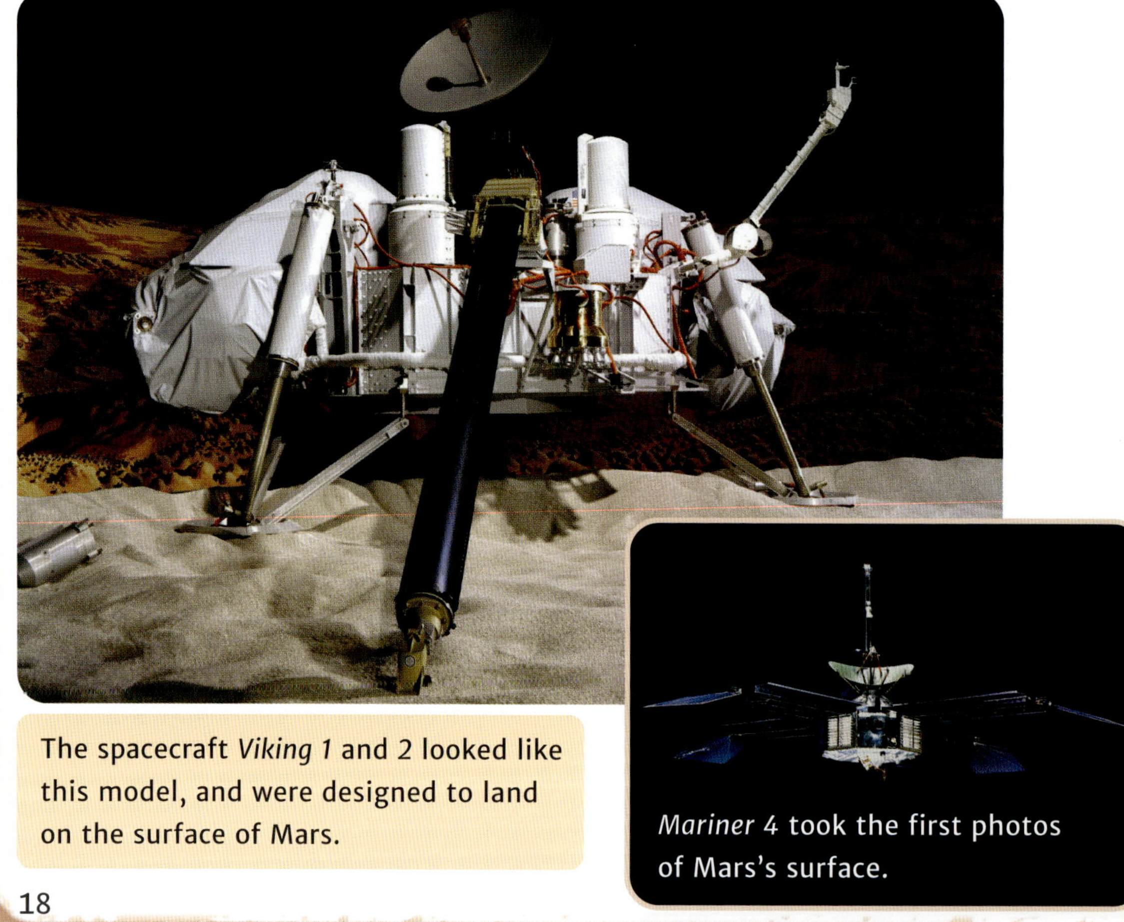

The spacecraft *Viking 1* and 2 looked like this model, and were designed to land on the surface of Mars.

Mariner 4 took the first photos of Mars's surface.

In the 1990s, the *Pathfinder* **rover**, called Sojourner, drove across the surface of Mars and studied its soil and rocks. It helped scientists to discover that Mars once had liquid water on its surface.

In the late 1990s, a number of remotely controlled spacecraft were sent to Mars. They orbited around Mars, studying its atmosphere as well as its surface and gathering information about the water there. They discovered that Mars has large **glaciers** and once had volcanoes.

The Sojourner rover drives across the surface of Mars, away from the *Pathfinder* lander.

The Perseverance Mission

In the first two decades of this century, a range of different Mars **missions** were launched by countries around the world, including the USA, India, China and the United Arab Emirates. Some missions sent vehicles to orbit Mars. Others sent vehicles to land on Mars and explore its surface.

One of the most important missions to Mars began in 2020, when the spacecraft carrying the Perseverance rover was launched from Cape Canaveral Air Force Station in Florida, USA. The rover landed on Mars on 18 February 2021.

NASA's Perseverance rover took this selfie on Mars in September 2021. The two holes in the rock in front of it were made using the drill on its robotic arm, while collecting samples.

The Perseverance rover is like a small **laboratory** on wheels. It can study the chemicals in the soil on the surface of Mars. It also has cameras and X-ray machines that allow it to search for signs of life that may once have existed on Mars. If signs of life are found, they will probably be tiny **organisms**, such as **bacteria**, rather than plants or animals.

The Perseverance rover can also collect rock samples. Scientists hope that one day they will be able to send a spacecraft to bring the samples back to Earth for closer study.

Scientists inserted sample tubes in the Perseverance rover's laboratory before it was sent to Mars. The rover's laboratory sits underneath its body.

The Exploration of Mars: A Timeline

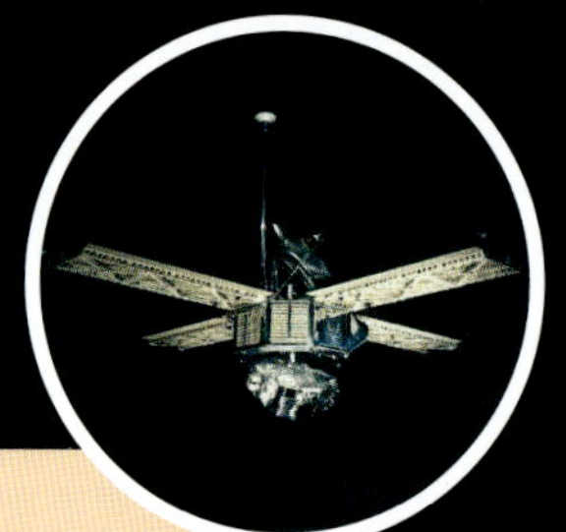

1969

***Mariner* 6 and 7** send back hundreds of photos of the surface of Mars.

1971

***Mariner* 9** takes photos of extinct volcanoes on Mars, as well as the first close-up photos of its moons.

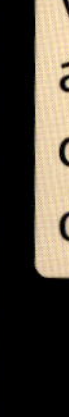

1996

Pathfinder lander and its rover, **Sojourner**, perform tests that show Mars used to have liquid water and a thicker atmosphere.

1964

***Mariner* 4** flies close enough to Mars to take photos of its craters and moons.

1975

***Viking* 1** and **2** land on Mars and conduct experiments on the soil to look for signs of life. ***Viking* 1** sends back the first photo ever taken on the surface of Mars.

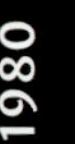

1990

2013

Mangalyaan orbiter, India's first mission to Mars, studies the surface and atmosphere of Mars.

2020

Tianwen 1, China's first Mars lander and its rover, **Zhurong**, study the Martian soil and hunt for underground water using radar.

2011

Mars Science Laboratory rover, nicknamed **Curiosity**, shows that Mars once had conditions that may have been suitable for life.

2007

Phoenix scout studies the ice and clouds of Mars.

2020

Perseverance rover studies Mars to assess if it is suitable for human habitation. It also looks for signs of simple life forms (organisms) that may have existed on Mars.

2000 2010 2020

Could Humans Live on Mars?

We do not yet have the technology to safely send humans to Mars. However, scientists believe that if humans are going to find somewhere else in the solar system to live, Mars would be the best place. Venus and Mercury are much too hot to support life.

Mars, however, has water in the form of ice. Although it gets very cold on Mars, it wouldn't be too cold for humans to survive indoors if they built shelters there. Furthermore, Mars has a thin atmosphere that offers some protection from radiation.

Mars gets a lot of sunlight, so humans would be able to use solar panels to produce electricity there.

It would take about seven months to fly to Mars from Earth, but as technology improves, this time is likely to decrease.

Companies like AI Spacefactory have designed imagined buildings that people could use to live on Mars.

Mars is an incredible planet. Missions to Mars, such as Perseverance, offer humans many opportunities to learn about space, and about the environments of other planets.

Even if we never visit in person or set up a **base** there, when we study Mars and other planets, we learn more about our own planet and how it came to exist. We learn to appreciate Earth's beauty, and its unique features that allow plants and animals to live and grow here. We are also reminded of the importance of taking care of Earth's environment.

Should Humans Set Up a Base on Mars?

Many people have strong opinions about whether or not humans should try to set up a permanent base on Mars.

Asma, 10

I think it would be a great idea for humans to set up a base on Mars.

First, Earth's environment would be much better off if large numbers of people moved to another planet. There are now so many people living on Earth that we are putting its natural resources under great pressure. Our demands for different types of fuel are creating pollution and causing damage to the fragile environments that support plant and animal life.

Furthermore, if humans decide to set up a base on Mars, this will drive us to make great advances in technology. Scientists will need to develop all sorts of new devices and materials to make life on Mars safe and comfortable.

In the past, research for space missions has resulted in many useful inventions. Some of these have benefitted people on Earth, too. For example, space researchers have invented new types of water filters. These can make dirty water safe to drink here on Earth.

Moving to Mars might also help us to find new ways of living together and cooperating with each other. For example, the cold weather and lack of oxygen on Mars would mean that we would need to stay inside most of the time. This would make us find new ways to live together peacefully and productively.

Artists are already creating works that imagine what a base on Mars would look like.

Connor, 10

I think it would be a really bad idea for humans to set up a base on Mars.

To begin with, it would be extremely expensive to build vehicles that could take humans all the way to Mars. The equipment and materials we would need to build a base there would be very expensive, too. I believe this money would be better spent looking after the environment here on Earth, and taking care of Earth's people, plants and animals.

Even if we made it to Mars, we might not enjoy living there. We would have to spend most of our time indoors, breathing conditioned air, which might not be healthy. It would also be difficult and expensive to produce healthy, fresh food on Mars.

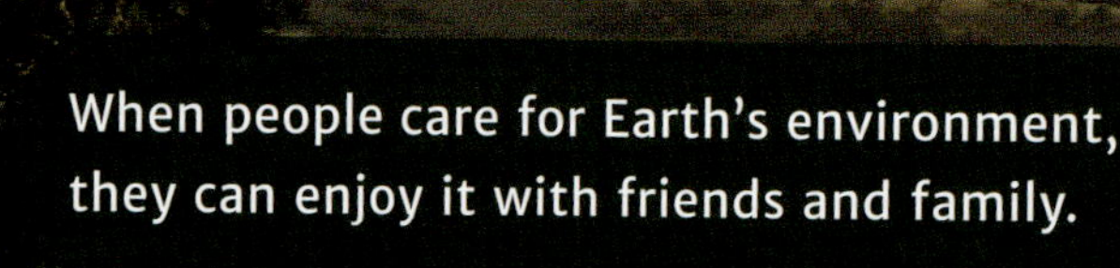

When people care for Earth's environment, they can enjoy it with friends and family.

Living so close together, people might struggle to get along. If anyone wanted to return to Earth, it would take them months to fly back here.

I think a human settlement on Mars could even be bad for Mars itself. We might end up damaging Mars's environment, like we've done to Earth's.

Clearly, there are many positive and negative aspects to setting up a base on Mars. We will have to think these issues through carefully as we prepare for future missions to Mars.

Glossary

astronomers (*noun*) scientists who study space and the things in it, such as stars and planets

atmosphere (*noun*) the layer of gases surrounding a planet

Babylonian (*adjective*) from ancient Babylonia, an area including present-day Syria and Iraq

bacteria (*noun*) tiny living things

base (*noun*) a place where people can stay and keep equipment

Celsius (adjective) on a scale for measuring temperature

diameter (*noun*) the distance from one side to the other through the centre of a sphere

elliptical (*adjective*) shaped like an oval or egg

extinct (*adjective*) no longer active or alive

galaxy (*noun*) a huge group of stars

glaciers (*noun*) rivers of solid ice that move very slowly

laboratory (*noun*) a place specially designed for scientific experiments

Martian (*adjective*) to do with Mars

missions (*noun*) trips to another place to carry out a task, usually scientific

NASA (*noun*) the National Aeronautics and Space Administration in the USA

observatory (*noun*) a building designed for observing land, seas or skies

orbiting (*verb*) continually circling around another object

organisms (*noun*) living things, such as animals, plants or bacteria

predict (*verb*) to make a guess about something that could happen in the future

rover (*noun*) a remote-controlled vehicle designed to explore the surface of a planet

solar system (*noun*) the group of planets and moons that orbit around the Sun

spherical (*adjective*) shaped like a ball or sphere

telescope (*noun*) an instrument that allows someone to look at distant objects

Index